Robert *Lives With His* Grandparents

Martha Whitmore Hickman
illustrated by Tim Hinton

Albert Whitman & Company • Morton Grove, Illinois

Library of Congress Cataloging-in-Publication Data

Hickman, Martha Whitmore.
Robert lives with his grandparents / written by Martha Whitmore Hickman;
illustrated by Tim Hinton.
p.   cm.
Summary: Robert is embarrassed to admit to his classmates that he has
lived with his grandparents ever since his parents' divorce.
ISBN 0-8075-7084-2
[1. Grandparents--Fiction. 2. Schools--Fiction.] I. Hinton, Tim, ill. II. Title.
PZ7.H53143Ro   1995   95-3122
[E]--dc20   CIP
                                                                  AC

The text is set in Bembo.
The illustrations are watercolor.
The design is by Karen Yops.

To the grandmothers who, thinking their stint is over,
pick up the tools of mothering once more
and tend another garden. M.W.H.

To Brian, to Danny McNeal, and to all
my children and nieces and nephews. T.H.

Robert Avery lived with his grandmother and grandfather in a house on Wilton Street. His room had sailboats on the wallpaper.

He had a blue bedspread and big pillows, a huge teddy bear, and a desk for his books and puzzles and his electronic baseball game. And he had his cat, Pretty Kitty, who wasn't pretty but that was her name.

Robert used to live with his mother and father on another street not far away. Then his parents got divorced, and his father moved away and never called or came to visit. His mother took more and more drugs, and she would go away and come back at all hours of the day and night.

One day his grandmother said to his mother, "We want Robert. Please let him come and live with us. Grandfather and I will take care of him and play with him and give him good food to eat and read books to him, and he will be like our very own little boy."

"I suppose so," his mother said. "If he wants to." She was sitting in a chair, looking sleepy and sad.

"How about it, Robert?" his grandparents asked him.

Robert looked into their faces. He knew they loved him very much. He had stayed with them many times. He would be safe. His friends could come and play. He knew that when his grandmother and grandfather said they would be there when he got home, they would be there. They would never go away and leave him alone, hour after hour after hour. But still . . .

"What about my mother?" he asked, looking at her.

"Your mother is not well, Robert," his grandmother said. "Your mother doesn't seem to know what she is doing. She is going away for awhile, to a place where they will help her not to need drugs anymore. When she gets better, she will come to visit."

"If I come to live with you, will my father know where I am?" he asked. "In case he comes?"

His grandmother smiled. "I'm sure he'll know where to look for you. He knows where we live," she said.

"I will come and live with you," Robert said. "For now, anyway."

So he did. He moved into the house on Wilton Street, into the room with sailboats on the wallpaper, the bed with the blue bedspread and big pillows, the huge teddy bear, and the desk for his books and puzzles and electronic baseball game. And his cat, Pretty Kitty, who wasn't pretty but that was her name.

"This is the room your mother slept in when she was a little girl," his grandmother said, straightening out the blankets on his bed.

"Oh," he said.

After his grandmother left the room he curled up on the bed and closed his eyes. He tried to think what it was like when his mother was a little girl in this same room where he lived now, and went to the same school where he was going—though of course his mother did not have Miss Abbott for a teacher.

Things were different in his grandparents' house. They had an upstairs and a downstairs, for one thing. They didn't want him to watch television or play video games as much as he was used to. But they had a basketball hoop in their driveway. They took him to the library on Saturdays, and they helped him with his homework if he asked them. And his grandmother fixed all his favorite foods.

He missed his mother and father, but he didn't miss their leaving him all alone or being mad for no reason or fighting all the time. In school when people asked about his parents, he pretended not to hear. When friends came over to play, he would take them to his room, or they would play outside. If someone saw his grandmother or grandfather and asked, "Who's that?" he would say, "My grandmother" or "My grandfather." He wouldn't tell that his mother and father didn't live there, too.

Then one day in school Miss Abbott announced, "Next week we're going to have Parents' Day." She gave out notices that said, "Parents: Please come and visit our school on Tuesday, November 15, between 2:00 and 3:30 or between 7:00 and 8:30." She said to the children, "Take these notices

home to your parents. We'll put up some of your artwork
along the walls. If your parents come in the afternoon, you
can show them where you sit in our classroom and show
them some of the things you're doing."

Every time he heard "parents," Robert felt his stomach drop a little farther. If people knew he didn't live with his parents . . .

His grandparents had wrinkles on their faces, and they even had gray hair. Though he loved them, he felt funny at the thought of their coming here with all the mothers and fathers with black hair and red hair and yellow hair and no wrinkles. He folded up the note and put it in his pocket. And when he got home he didn't show it to anyone.

But two days later when his grandmother went to do the wash, she found the note in his pocket. When he came home from school, she said, "Robert, you forgot to give me this note. I'll be glad to come. Your grandfather will be at work, of course, but I'd like to come in the afternoon so I can see you in your classroom."

Uh, oh. Now everybody will know, he thought. But he loved his grandmother and wouldn't hurt her feelings for the world. So he said, "Okay, Grandma. That will be fine"— even though his heart was sinking.

The next Tuesday came, and sure enough, soon after 2:00 his grandmother walked in, along with some mothers and fathers. Miss Abbott welcomed them all. "Boys and girls," she said, "would you come and show your parents some of the work you've done that's hanging on the boards?"

Robert stood up with the other children whose families had come. He walked over to his grandmother and took her hand. She smiled at him. "Hi, Robert," she whispered. When they got as far as Miss Abbott, she said to the teacher, "You know, I'm Robert's grandmother. I'm very proud of Robert."

"Of course," Miss Abbott said. She turned to the class.
"Everyone, this is Robert's grandmother. Who thinks Robert
is lucky to have a grandmother coming to Open House?"
All the hands shot up.
Robert looked at the boys and girls. They were looking

at him and his grandmother with normal smiling faces.

"Is there something you'd like to tell us about your grandmother, Robert?" the teacher asked. "We're so happy to have a grandmother here, aren't we, children?"

"Yes!" they all answered.

"My grandmother made the cookies I brought for the Halloween party," he said. The children smiled again, remembering. Then he added, "I live with my grandmother and grandfather. They take care of me and Pretty Kitty—who isn't pretty but that's her name."

The children laughed.

"Is anyone else's grandmother coming to Open House?" Miss Abbott asked.

No one answered right away, but then Heather Cramer put her hand up. "I live with my grandmother, too," she said.

Up in the front row, Billy Merita raised his hand. "I live with my Aunt Maggie," he said. "She's coming to Open House tonight."

Robert couldn't believe his ears. He wasn't the only one at all!

45
+11
52
+7
81
+71
NEXT WEEK
ASSIGNMEN
HAVE TWO CENT
ARE GOOD FRIEN

Miss Abbott was talking to his grandmother. "Maybe you'll be one of our class grandmothers," Miss Abbott said.

"Yeah!" the children called out.

Robert's grandmother smiled. "What does a class grandmother do?" she asked.

"Just come and visit us once in a while," the teacher said. "Would that be all right?"

"I'll be glad to," Robert's grandmother said, "if it's all right with Robert."

"Sure," Robert said, and he really meant it, too.

Then Miss Abbott introduced each of the parents. Everyone walked around, talking and exploring the classroom.

Soon the clock said 3:30.

"Well," said Miss Abbott to everyone, "we've had a very nice day. And now it's time to go home."

So all the grownups and all the children put on their coats. They said "Thank you" to Miss Abbott, and she said, "Thank you for coming."

They all went outside. Robert held his grandmother's hand, and they walked down the road toward home, where Grandfather and Pretty Kitty were waiting.

MARTHA WHITMORE HICKMAN lives with her husband in Nashville, Tennessee. She says, "I loved my role as a mother of young children, and I love being a grandparent. But I stand in awe and compassion before anyone who has to be both at once!"

She is the author of more than twenty books for adults and children. Her recent books for children include *When Andy's Father Went to Prison* and *And God Created Squash: How the World Began.*

TIM HINTON is a nationally recognized artist whose works have been exhibited in the Museum of African Art, the Smithsonian Anacostia Museum, and the Kennedy Center as well as several other museum and corporate collections. His historical art prints are displayed in all the national monuments in Washington, D.C.

This is Mr. Hinton's first book for children. He lives with his wife and three children in Upper Marlboro, Maryland.